No Copycats Allowed!

Bonnie Graves

Illustrated by Abby Carter

Hyperion Books for Children
New York

Printed in the United States of America.

First Edition

1 3 5 7 9 10 8 6 4 2

The artwork for each picture is prepared using pen and ink.
The text for this book is set in 16-point Berkeley Old Style.

Library of Congress Cataloging-in-Publication Data
Graves, Bonnie B.
No copycats allowed! / Bonnie Graves. — 1st ed.
p.   cm.
Summary: Starting at a new school, Gabrielle tries to make new friends while struggling with the spelling of her long name.
ISBN 0-7868-1166-8 (trade) — ISBN 0-7868-2235-X (lib. bdg.)
[1. Schools—Fiction. 2. Names, Personal—Fiction. 3. Friendship—Fiction.]
I. Title
PZ7.G77515Ho   1998
[E]—dc21   97-18048

For my mother,
who named me,
and, of course,
Gabrielle
—B. G.

No Copycats Allowed!

Contents

Chapter 1

Mean Mrs. Dean

"I'm not going in," Gabrielle Gilbert told Dillon at the door to Room 6.

"It'll be okay. Just watch out for mean Mrs. Dean and do what everyone else does," her big brother told her. Dillon opened the door and gave Gabrielle a little shove into the noisy room.

Gabrielle felt icky, as if the Cocoa

Crunchies she had had for breakfast were exploding inside her stomach. Why did her family have to move from the city to the suburbs, anyway?

Room 6 was already full of kids . . . and desks, tables, computers, and books. Pictures covered the walls. Pictures of animals and people and places Gabrielle

had never seen before. All around there were words printed in black ink, too. Gabrielle read the words, WELCOME SECOND GRADERS.

Gabrielle looked around for the teacher. She spotted a woman with white hair sitting at a piano. A bunch of kids stood around her. Could this be mean Mrs. Dean?

Gabrielle rubbed her fingers over the fuzzy soft yarn of the sweater Granny Gilbert had knitted for her. She was glad she had worn it, even though it wasn't cold today. It smelled like Granny and felt almost like a hug.

Gabrielle walked over to the white-haired lady. On her way she peeked into a box next to the piano. Tambourines, triangles, brightly colored shakers, and a bunch of other instruments! If only . . . if only she had her dad's shiny silver trumpet with her! Gabrielle could play her dad's trumpet . . . almost. He was teaching her.

Gabrielle tapped the shoulder of the lady at the piano bench. "Are you the teacher?" Gabrielle asked.

The lady turned around. "That I am. My name is Mrs. Dean." Mrs. Dean had wrinkles and smelled like soap. "And what is your name?" she asked in a loud voice.

"Gabrielle," Gabrielle said loudly, too. She loved her name. She loved the way her name felt on her lips and her tongue. She loved the way it sounded, "Gab-re-EL."

Mrs. Dean's blue eyes twinkled. "Are you wearing the name tag I sent, Gabrielle?"

Gabrielle unbuttoned her sweater to show her teacher the name tag.

A boy wearing a baseball cap laughed. "That's a *long* name!"

Gabrielle smiled. "Nine letters."

"Too long," said the boy with the cap. His name tag read TOM.

A girl with carrot-colored braids asked, "How do you say it?" Her name tag read LIBBY.

"Gab-re-EL," Gabrielle said.

"What kind of name is that?" asked a boy with a jillion freckles and the name tag ROB. "I've never heard of it."

Mrs. Dean started to play the piano and sing:

Welcome, welcome, old friends and new.
Quickly, quietly
Ska-diddle, ska-dat
Find a place on the rug
And we'll have a chat.

After all the kids sat on the rug, Mrs. Dean said, "I gave each of you a name tag because names are very important. We will wear our name tags until everyone learns everyone else's name and how to spell it, too. Then we'll have a name tag party."

"What kind of party is that?" Tom asked.

"We'll play a game where everybody spells everybody else's name. And I want each of you to bring something to share, something that tells something special about you." Mrs. Dean looked right at Gabrielle and smiled.

Gabrielle smiled back. She knew just what she was going to bring!

"We'll have cookies and ice cream, too," Mrs. Dean said.

"Yum!" Gabrielle blurted. "I love ice cream!"

The freckle-faced boy named Rob

pointed at Gabrielle. "I'll never be able to spell that girl's name."

"Me, either," said the boy in the baseball cap. "Maybe you could change it."

Never! thought Gabrielle.

Chapter 2

Gabrielle

"I'm NOT going to change my name," Gabrielle told her dad at breakfast the next morning.

"Change your name? Why would you change your name?" he asked, sticking her name tag onto her T-shirt.

"The kids in my new room think it's weird."

"No way! Gabrielle's a beautiful name. Everybody at Hale liked it," Dad told her.

"The kids at Hale were nice," Gabrielle said. She thought of her best friends Olivia, Lottie, and Danika. Mr. Shively had called them the "G-O-L-D-en" girls.

"Well, I'm sure the kids at Morningside are nice, too. Just give them a chance," said Mr. Gilbert.

"Wrong, Dad," Dillon broke in. "My two new friends, Stubbs and Howie, say the kids in Room 6 are mean." And he made a face to show how mean they were.

"See?" Gabrielle said.

"Dillon's just being a pest," Dad said.

Gabrielle scrunched up her nose at Dillon and stuck out her chin. "Mrs. Dean's nice, though," she told her dad. "She plays the piano and has tambourines and triangles and lots of other stuff that kids can play. Can I take your trumpet to school? Please?"

"No," said Dad.

"But . . ."

"Sorry, Gabrielle. That horn's my bread and butter."

When grown-ups said *bread and butter,* Gabrielle knew it meant something very important.

Mr. Gilbert played in a band at night. Gabrielle's mom taught music at the high school in the morning. Dillon played the drums morning, noon, and night.

When Gabrielle left for the bus, Mr. Gilbert gave her a big hug and said, "Just be yourself, and you'll make lots of friends. You'll see. You don't need any old horn." He rumpled her black-as-pepper curls.

"No way. Be like everybody else!" Dillon yelled as he raced by her. "Or you *won't* make friends!"

Dillon had already made two friends at

Morningside. Maybe he knew something she didn't.

Before Gabrielle got to the bus stop, she buttoned her sweater over her name tag.

Chapter 3

Libby

As soon as Gabrielle got off the bus, Libby, the girl in Room 6 with the carrot-colored braids, skipped up to her.

Libby stared at Gabrielle's name tag. "What's your name again?" Libby asked. "It's hard to read."

"Gab-re-EL," Gabrielle told her, beginning to hate her name and hate her

new school. Gabrielle's feet started toward the building, but she wanted to run home.

Libby walked beside Gabrielle. "Gab-re-EL," she repeated. "That's a cool name."

Gabrielle turned to look at Libby. "Really?"

"Yeah. Did you make it up?"

"No! I'm named after my aunt Gabrielle

from England. She writes books."

"Cool!" said Libby. "I want to write books, too. Really scary ones. Want to trade?" Libby asked.

"Trade?"

"Names."

Gabrielle shrugged. Why not? She peeled off her name tag and gave it to Libby.

Libby put Gabrielle's name tag on her T-shirt. "You want to be a writer, too, like your aunt Gabrielle?" Libby smiled. She had small pointy teeth.

"No, I'm going to be a—ouch!" Gabrielle said.

Dillon bounced a basketball on the top of her head. Then he ran up the steps of Morningside Elementary with his two new friends—Stubbs and Howie.

"So what do you want to be?" Libby asked.

She thought of what Dillon had said that morning. *Be like everybody else! Or you won't make friends!*

"I want to be a, ah . . . ," Gabrielle knew what she wanted to be, but maybe Dillon was right. Maybe she should try to be like the other kids. Maybe that's what it took to have friends at Morningside.

"I mean, yes, I want to be a writer, too," she said.

"Cool," said Libby, hopping up the steps. "Maybe we can write books together. Scary ones like *Goosebumps*." She opened the school door and started skipping down the hall toward Room 6. Gabrielle skipped beside her.

* * *

At work time, Gabrielle practiced writing Libby's name for the name tag party.

She especially liked the *y*. She liked the way it sounded like an *e*.

Gabrielle had an *e* at the end of it, but the *e* had no sound at all.

If Gabrielle had a *y* in her name, she would make the tail very long and looped. You could do lots of things with a *y*, she decided.

When she tried writing her name with a *y* and two *b*s, like Libby, she liked the way it looked. G-a-b-b-y.

She liked the way it sounded. GAB-ee.

It reminded her of Libby with the orange braids.

Libby was a little weird, but nice. They could be best friends. Twins almost. Libby and Gabby. They could write books. Scary ones.

Yes, she would change her name to Gabby. It was perfect.

After work time Gabrielle told Libby, "I learned how to spell your name," and she handed Libby her name tag.

"I learned how to spell yours, too," Libby said proudly. She smiled and peeled off Gabrielle's name tag. "Here," she said.

"Keep it," Gabrielle told her. "I decided to change my name to Gabby."

"You did? Cool," said Libby.

Gabrielle put Libby's name tag back on Libby's T-shirt.

"What should I do with GABRIELLE?" Libby asked.

Gabrielle shrugged.

"Can I keep it?" Libby asked.

"Sure."

Gabrielle skipped off to ask Mrs. Dean for a new name tag. On it, she wrote:

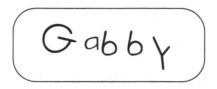

Gabrielle smiled at her new name. Morningside was turning out okay after all. She had been here for only one day and one hour, and she had a new friend, Libby, and a new name, Gabby!

Chapter 4

Addie

When it was time for art, Gabrielle saw Libby sitting next to a girl with two red bows in her hair. Her name tag read ADDIE.

Gabrielle found paper and crayons and sat across from Libby and Addie. Maybe she could make *two* new friends today!

But Addie didn't even look at Gabrielle.

Neither did Libby. Addie was busy drawing. Libby was busy leaning over Addie's picture.

"You draw really good," Libby told Addie.

"I can draw good, too," said Gabrielle in a loud voice. But Libby didn't look up. Addie didn't stop drawing.

"I'm going to be an artist when I grow up," Addie told Libby.

"I'm going to be an artist, too," said Gabrielle in an even louder voice.

Addie stopped drawing and stared at Gabrielle. "Really?" said Addie. "Awesome."

Libby gave Gabrielle an odd look. "I thought you were going to be a writer," she said.

"Oh," Gabrielle said. "Well, a writer and an artist."

Gabrielle watched Addie sign her name on her picture. She gave the *e* a long tail that flipped over the *e* to dot the *i*. If Gabrielle spelled her name G-a-b-b-i-e, she could dot the *i* the same way.

During work time Gabrielle practiced writing her name the new way. It sounded just like G-a-b-b-y. But she decided she liked the way the *ie* looked. It was fun dotting the *i* with the tail of the *e*. It looked very artistic.

Gabrielle asked Mrs. Dean for a new name tag. On it she wrote:

Gabbie

Gabrielle smiled at her new name. Her second day at Morningside School and she had two new names, Gabby and Gabbie, and two new friends—Libby and Addie!

Chapter 5

Debi

At lunchtime, Gabrielle saw Libby and Addie sitting on the grass with another girl.

"Hi!" Gabrielle walked over to the three girls and sat down. The new girl's name tag said DEBI.

"In my old school in Georgia," Debi was saying, "we all put on a play each month. It was really fun."

"Cool!" said Libby.

"Awesome," said Addie.

"You talk really neat," Gabrielle told Debi. Debi's voice made Gabrielle think of faraway places. Her words sounded almost like music. "I like the way you spell your name, too," Gabrielle said.

"I'm named after a movie star. You know, Debi Dupont? Except I want to be like Judy Garland. You know, from *The Wizard of Oz?*"

Debi *looked* like a movie star. She had long dark hair and wore earrings.

Gabrielle decided it would be nice to have Debi for a friend, too. And it might be fun to be a movie star. She would make lots of money. Everyone would know her. She could write her name G-a-b-i.

"I'm going to be a movie star, too," Gabrielle told Debi.

"You told me you wanted to be a writer," said Libby.

"I thought you were going to be an artist," said Addie.

"Maybe I'll be all three!" said Gabrielle.

* * *

After lunch recess, Gabrielle practiced writing her name the new way. G-a-b-i sounded like Gabby and Gabbie, but it looked more exciting.

If she were a movie star, she would sign her name with a little heart over the *i*.

At the end of the day Gabrielle asked Mrs. Dean for a new name tag.

"Another name tag?" Mrs. Dean asked. "You're changing your name again?"

"No, just the spelling!"

Mrs. Dean gave Gabrielle another name tag. On it Gabrielle wrote:

$$\boxed{\text{Gabi}}$$

"Now I have three new ways to spell my name—G-a-b-b-y, G-a-b-b-i-e, and G-a-b-i. And three new things to be—a writer, an artist, and a movie star. And I have three new friends—Libby, Addie, and Debi!" Gabrielle told Mrs. Dean. "You can call us the G-L-A-D girls!"

Mrs. Dean smiled. "Well, don't forget your name tag tomorrow. I can't wait to see what name you choose and what you bring for show-and-tell!"

Uh-oh! Show-and-tell. She had forgotten about that! What was she going to bring? And what name *was* she going to choose?

Chapter 6

Gabby, Gabbie, or Gabi?

The next morning Gabrielle felt all bubbly inside. She jumped out of bed. Today at school she was going to have a party with her three new friends—Libby, Addie, and Debi. She could hardly wait!

Gabrielle stepped into her jeans and pulled on a T-shirt. Then she scooped her name tags off her dresser—Gabby, Gabbie, and Gabi. Which name should she choose?

Wait a minute! Why choose just one when she could be all three at once? She stuck the three names to her T-shirt— GABBY, GABBIE, and GABI.

Then Gabrielle had another wonderful idea. She ran to the basement where her mom kept the Christmas wrapping stuff and snipped off two lengths of red ribbon.

Gabrielle took the ribbons to her dad. "Can you braid my hair? Two pigtails?" *Pigtails like Libby!*

Mr. Gilbert looked at Gabrielle's short, pepper-colored curls.

"Too short, Gab. They'll stick out from your head."

"I don't care," said Gabrielle. "And put these on them." She handed him the red ribbons. *Ribbons like Addie!*

Dad braided Gabrielle's hair and tied the ribbons on. The braids stuck out from her head.

With her fingers, she felt the stiff little tails and the slippery ribbons. "Cool," she said.

Dillon whizzed by and yanked a tail. "Oink, oink," he said. "Cute little piggy."

"Stop it!" she screamed. "Dad, can I borrow Mom's earrings, please?"

"No way!" Dad said.

"Please, please, p-l-e-a-s-e?"

"No, no, N-O."

Gabrielle ran to her room. With a red marking pen she drew two little circles on her earlobes. She looked at herself in the mirror. "Awesome," she said. *Earrings like Debi!*

She grabbed the bag with her show-and-
tell. She could hardly wait to get to school!

Chapter 7

Copycat

When Gabrielle got to school, Libby, Addie, and Debi were huddled together on the playground near the climbing bars. When they saw her running over to join them, they yelled, "Here comes Copycat!" They laughed and ran off.

Copycat? Gabrielle ran after them. "What do you mean?" she yelled. But they didn't

answer. They just kept on running. "Hey, wait up!" Gabrielle tripped on a bump in the blacktop. Her bag flew from her hand and her show-and-tell spilled onto the playground: "The Advenshurs of the 4 Friends" (the story she had written), her drawing of the G-L-A-D girls, and a picture of Judy Garland she had cut from a magazine.

Before "The Advenshurs of the 4 Friends" could blow away, she picked it up and tore it to pieces. She did the same with her drawing and the picture of Judy Garland. Then she threw all the pieces in the trash and ran from the school yard.

As Gabrielle ran down the sidewalk, she untied the red ribbons and pulled the rubber bands from her pigtails. She couldn't get home fast enough. She hated Morningside School. Dillon was right after all. The kids in Room 6 *were* mean.

Gabrielle had a long way to run. But she knew the way. It was the way the bus went. She wished she could run back to Hale. Back to Olivia, Lottie, and Danika. Back to G-O-L-D.

When Gabrielle got to her street, she was out of breath. And then she heard something. Her dad's trumpet. The notes reached all the way to the end of the block. They pulled her home like a magnet.

"I hate that school, and I'm not going back," she screamed as she opened the door and ran inside.

Mr. Gilbert put down his trumpet. "Gabrielle! What the . . . What happened?"

"It's a horrible school. Dillon was right. The kids are mean! Mean! Mean! Mean!"

"But you can't just leave! Tell me. What happened?"

Gabrielle crawled into her dad's lap and told him the whole story. And then she said, "They called me *Copycat* and ran off."

"Boy, that's mean, all right," her dad said,

rubbing her back. "I'd be just as mad as you are."

"You would?" Gabrielle turned to look into her father's face.

"You bet."

"So you'd run away and wouldn't go back?" Gabrielle asked.

"I might run away, but I'd go back. Yep, I'd go back for sure."

"Why? They're just going to be mean again."

"Maybe, maybe not."

"Well, I'm not going back. Ever!"

Chapter 8

What to Do?

In her room, Gabrielle looked at herself in the full length mirror on her closet door. The three name tags still clung to her T-shirt:

Gabby

Gabbie

Gabi

Copycat! She heard Libby's and Addie's and Debi's voices yell inside her head. *Copycat!* A tear trickled down her cheek. Libby, Addie, and Debi were mean, but they were right. That's exactly what she was—a copycat. She hadn't meant to be, but she was. Libby, Addie, and Debi might be right, but they were still mean. And she didn't want mean people for friends. No way.

"Look what I found," Dad said, standing at the bedroom door.

Quickly Gabrielle wiped her eyes with the back of her hand. "What's that?" she asked.

"A blank name tag left from a meeting at Mom's school."

"So?"

"For the name tag party. Mrs. Dean

called. She's worried about you, and so are your friends."

"They're not my friends."

"Well, that's what she called them."

"Who?"

"Libby, Addie, and Debi," Dad said. "Mrs. Dean called you the G-L-A-D girls."

"She did?"

"Uh-huh. They want you to come to the name tag party."

"Who?"

"Libby, Addie, and Debi," Dad said.

"They do?"

"Yep. And Mrs. Dean said you're having cookies and ice cream."

"Ice cream before lunch?"

"That's what Mrs. Dean said."

"And show-and-tell?"

"That's what she said."

"Dad?"

"Yep?"

"Can I bring your trumpet? Please?"

Chapter 9

Show-and-tell

"Gabrielle!" Mrs. Dean said as Gabrielle and her dad walked into the room. "You're just in time. We're starting our name tag game and show-and-tell. Then we'll have refreshments. Come and sit down. You, too, Mr. Gilbert."

Gabrielle and her dad found empty chairs at the back of the room, and Mrs. Dean started the show-and-tell.

"When I call on you, show us what you brought, then take off your name tag and everyone will spell your name."

Libby was first. She showed a book she had written. It had a fancy cover with her name on it.

"Wonderful, Libby," said Mrs. Dean. "Now take off your name tag. How do you spell Libby, class?"

"L-i-b-b-y," everyone said.

Addie was second. She held up a brightly colored paper collage.

"Beautiful, Addie," said Mrs. Dean.

Addie peeled off her name tag.

"How do you spell Addie, class?"

"A-d-d-i-e."

Debi was third. She showed a picture of Judy Garland with The Scarecrow, The Lion, and The Tin Man.

"Very nice, Debi," said Mrs. Dean. "And how do you spell Debi, class?"

"D-e-b-i!"

Then Mrs. Dean's eyes found Gabrielle at the back of the room.

Gabrielle stared back at her. She looked at Libby and Addie and Debi. They looked more like enemies than friends.

"Would you like to be next?" Mrs. Dean asked Gabrielle.

Gabrielle picked up her show-and-tell bag and walked to the front of the class. All the kids stared at her. Good. She pulled the trumpet out of her bag and blew, strong and loud, her fingers pressing the notes like her dad had taught her. "When the Saints Go Marching In!" The melody bounced off the walls and back again.

"Wow," Mrs. Dean said, and she clapped

her hands. So did the rest of Room 6. A few kids even whistled.

When the noise settled down, Gabrielle said, "I'm going to be a trumpet player when I grow up and have my own band."

"How wonderful," Mrs. Dean said. "We will all look forward to that. And now, class, how do you spell . . . ," Mrs. Dean looked for Gabrielle's name tag. It was hidden under her sweater.

"Gabrielle," Gabrielle said. "How do you spell Gab-re-EL?"

No one said a word. The room was so quiet Gabrielle could hear her heart beating inside her chest.

Then a small voice started to spell out her name. It was Libby. "G-a-b-r-i-e-l-l-e."

Then Addie chimed in a bit louder. "G-a-b-r-i-e-l-l-e."

"G-a-b-r-i-e-l-l-e," said Debi clearly in her musical voice.

"Gab-re-EL," Gabrielle repeated with Mrs. Dean and the rest of the class.

How wonderful her name felt on her lips and her tongue.

How wonderful it sounded when her new friends said it.

"Gabrielle."

Enjoy More Hyperion Chapter Books!

ALISON'S PUPPY

SPY IN THE SKY

SOLO GIRL

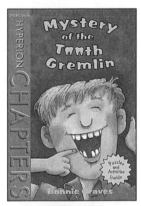

**MYSTERY OF
THE TOOTH GREMLIN**

**MY SISTER
THE SAUSAGE ROLL**

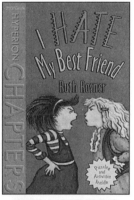

I HATE MY BEST FRIEND

**ALISON'S FIERCE AND
UGLY HALLOWEEN**

SECONDHAND STAR

GRACE THE PIRATE

Hyperion Chapters

2nd Grade
Alison's Fierce and Ugly Halloween
Alison's Puppy
Alison's Wings
The Banana Split from Outer Space
Edwin and Emily
Emily at School
The Peanut Butter Gang
Scaredy Dog
Sweets & Treats: Dessert Poems

2nd/3rd Grade
The Best, Worst Day
I Hate My Best Friend
Jenius: The Amazing Guinea Pig
Jennifer, Too
The Missing Fossil Mystery
Mystery of the Tooth Gremlin
No Copycats Allowed!
No Room for Francie
Pony Trouble
Princess Josie's Pets
Secondhand Star
Solo Girl
Spoiled Rotten

3rd Grade
Behind the Couch
Christopher Davis's Best Year Yet
Eat!
Grace the Pirate
The Kwanzaa Contest
The Lighthouse Mermaid
Mamá's Birthday Surprise
My Sister the Sausage Roll
Racetrack Robbery
Spy in the Sky
Third Grade Bullies